WORLD CULTURES

Aboriginal Australians

DIANA MARSHALL

MEDIA ENHANCED BOOKS
AV2 BY WEIGL
ADDED VALUE • AUDIO VISUAL

www.av2books.com

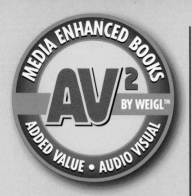

AV² provides enriched content that supplements and complements this book. Weigl's AV² books strive to create inspired learning and engage young minds in a total learning experience.

Your AV² Media Enhanced books come alive with...

Go to **www.av2books.com**, and enter this book's unique code.

BOOK CODE

Q 3 3 1 6 1 5

AV² by Weigl brings you media enhanced books that support active learning.

Audio
Listen to sections of the book read aloud.

Video
Watch informative video clips.

Embedded Weblinks
Gain additional information for research.

Try This!
Complete activities and hands-on experiments.

Key Words
Study vocabulary, and complete a matching word activity.

Quizzes
Test your knowledge.

Slide Show
View images and captions, and prepare a presentation.

... and much, much more!

Published by AV² by Weigl
350 5th Avenue, 59th Floor
New York, NY 10118
Website: www.av2books.com   www.weigl.com

Library of Congress Cataloging-in-Publication Data
Marshall, Diana.
 Aboriginal Australians / Diana Marshall.
   p. cm. -- (World cultures)
 Includes index.
 ISBN 978-1-61913-093-7 (hard cover : alk. paper) -- ISBN 978-1-61913-528-4 (soft cover : alk. paper)
 1. Aboriginal Australians--History--Juvenile literature. 2. Aboriginal Australians--Social life and customs--Juvenile literature. I. Title.
 DU123.4.M38 2012
 305.89'915--dc23
                          2011050249

Printed in the United States of America in North Mankato, Minnesota
1 2 3 4 5 6 7 8 9 0 16 15 14 13 12

062012
WEP170512

Editor   Aaron Carr
Art Director   Terry Paulhus

CONTENTS

Where in the World?

Indian Ocean

Kimberley
Plateau

Tanami Desert

Great Sandy
Desert

AUSTRALIA

MacDonnell Ranges

Musgrave Range

Great Barrier Reef

Great Dividing Range

Great Dividing Range

South Australian Basin

ASIA

PACIFIC
OCEAN

INDIAN
OCEAN

AUSTRALIA

ANTARCTICA

SCALE

0   500 Miles

0   500 Kilometers

N
W   E
S

Population: about 22 million
Indigenous Population:
  about 517,000
Continent: Australia
States: Western Australia,
  South Australia,
  Queensland, New South
  Wales, Tasmania, Victoria
Territories: Northern
  Territory, Australian
  Capital Territory
Area: 2,966,153 square
  miles (7,682,300
  square kilometers)

The word "aboriginal" means the first people to inhabit a land. It is also the name of the **indigenous peoples** of Australia. These Aboriginal Australians are believed to have occupied every region of the **continent**, at one time or another, for more than 50,000 years. Today, Aboriginal Australians live in all states and territories of Australia, with the highest number living in the states of Queensland and New South Wales.

Many different theories explain how Aboriginal Australians first arrived in Australia. Some people believe that a group of people traveled from India to Australia using rafts and canoes thousands of years ago. Sea levels lowered during the last Ice Age, making the distance between Asia and Australia much shorter and easier to cross. Other people believe the water levels were so low that a bridge of land connected Southeast Asia to Australia.

Before the arrival of Europeans, Aboriginal Australians did not have a formal system of land ownership. They did not mark their territories because all members of the group knew the boundaries.

Aboriginal Australians believe that their people have always lived in Australia. The first inhabitants of Australia made a home on its sandy coasts and in its harsh deserts by adapting to the land.

Until 200 years ago, Aboriginal Australians were **nomadic**. They understood their environment, and they could survive in the harshest places in Australia. Since the arrival of European settlers in the late 1700s, Aboriginal Australians have been pushed out of the milder climates along the coast. Now, they live in the harsh regions known as "the **outback**." In these regions, Aboriginal Australians have learned how to find water in the desert and hunt animals in the bush land and forests.

Culture Cues

🦘 Australia is the smallest continent, but it is the sixth-largest country in the world.

🦘 It is estimated that by the year 2021, there will be more than 700,000 Aboriginal Australians. By 2016, it is projected that Queensland will overtake New South Wales as the state with the largest indigenous population in Australia.

🦘 Australia is almost as large as the United States, but it only has a population of about 21.7 million. The United States is home to more than 310 million people.

🦘 The capital of Australia is Canberra. The largest city is Sydney. In 1789, almost half of Sydney's Aboriginal population was wiped out by a smallpox epidemic.

Stories and Legends

Aboriginal culture is based on the concept of the "Dreamtime." The Dreamtime is the time when all things on Earth were created. During the Dreamtime, the **Ancestor** Spirits journeyed across the wasteland that was Earth. As they traveled across the land, they created animals, land, plants, the Moon, the sky, stars, the Sun, and water. When the spirits were finished, they changed into animals, plants, and other objects found on Earth. The places where the spirits settled are known as Dreaming Places. They form the environment in which Aboriginal Australians live. The Dreamtime creation stories explain the origin of the natural world and why these indigenous peoples should live in harmony with nature.

Koalas are featured in a number of Aboriginal Australian stories. The word "koala" is said to mean "no drink" in some Aboriginal languages.

Different Aboriginal groups have their own versions of the Dreamtime stories. Each group's stories and beliefs are called "Dreaming."

Although the stories are different, they share many of the same Ancestor Spirits. Creation stories often tell of a powerful father figure, known as Biami. He was the main creator who watched over his people, punishing those who broke his laws. During **initiation ceremonies**, Biami spoke to Aboriginal boys who were about to become men. Most Aboriginal groups tell the story of the Rainbow Serpent (also called Great Rainbow Snake or Mother Snake), a creator associated with water and new life. It is believed that as the Rainbow Serpent awoke from her long sleep at the center of Earth, her massive body created tracks in the dirt, which were filled with the rain of her magic. These tracks became lakes, rivers, and **billabongs**. With this water came growth and life.

Indigenous Australians believe there are many Ancestor Spirits, such as animal spirits, evil spirits, good spirits, land spirits, plant spirits, and sky spirits. Through the Dreamtime stories, Aboriginal Australians are able to understand how they are related to all other species and objects on Earth.

Birds frequently appear in the Dreamtime stories told by Aboriginal Australians. The colorful rainbow lorikeet is native to Australia.

THE STORY OF
The Emu, The Possum, and The Kangaroo

Long ago, an emu named Waitch and his uncle, a kangaroo named Quorra, lived together. They often argued about who was the better hunter. The elders decided they should hold a hunting contest to settle the matter. A possum named Koormal would be the prey.

At dawn on the chosen day, Waitch and Quorra set out on the great possum hunt. Quorra was the first to spot Koormal who was in an old gum tree. He quickly trapped the possum and returned home. When Waitch learned he had lost the contest, he became very angry.

After the contest, the elders met and decided to **banish** Waitch for his poor sportsmanship. Quorra felt sorry for his nephew and asked that he be banished as well. Today, all three animals live alone in nature.

Early Aboriginal Australians survived by fishing, gathering plant foods, and hunting birds, reptiles, and mammals. Early Aboriginal Australians were resourceful people who adapted their lifestyle to fit each new region and climate. As a result, Aboriginal groups were able to spread across the continent. Each group had its own territory and developed its own language, rituals, and social organizations.

When European settlers began landing on the sandy beaches of Australia in 1788, the indigenous peoples' way of life was disrupted. At the time, there were as many as one million Aboriginal Australians calling the island of Australia home. They belonged to 500 distinct groups and spoke nearly 250 different languages. Today, they speak 145 languages. Of these languages, about 110 are in danger of dying out. This is because many languages are spoken rarely, or only phrases or words remain in use.

European exploration of the island caused the loss of many Aboriginal Australians' lives and traditions. The first European settlement was in the area now known as Sydney. At first, contact with Europeans was peaceful.

Timeline of Aboriginal Australians

1788 The first European **colony** to be established on the island is made up of prisoners from Great Britain.

10,000–40,000 BC Aboriginal Australians arrive in Australia.

1770 Captain James Cook claims Australia for Great Britain when he lands in eastern Australia.

16th and 17th Century Dutch, Spanish, French, and British ships sail into Australian waters and survey the area.

However, the Europeans did not know much about the Aboriginal Australians' way of life, and soon, the two cultures began to fight. European settlers spread new diseases, killing many Aboriginal Australians. New animals were introduced to the land. These animals, such as sheep and cows, dirtied waterholes and destroyed many of the food sources Aboriginal Australians needed to survive. Many Aboriginal Australians were driven away from their homes and treated like wild animals. Aboriginal Australians were denied the right to practice their own cultural traditions. British settlers built villages in the best areas that had clean water, fertile land, and fish. Since Aboriginal Australians had not built permanent houses or farmed the land, Great Britain claimed Australia as a colony.

Many Aboriginal Australians tried to defend themselves using force. Traditional weapons used by Aboriginal Australians were no match for the British and their guns. Many Aboriginal Australians died while trying to protect their homes. One group of British settlers set up camp on the island of Tasmania in 1803. By 1820, many of the island's Aboriginal peoples had been killed or removed.

1967 Aboriginal Australians are able to become Australian citizens.

1876 The Tasmanian Aboriginal Australians officially disappear with the death of the last islander.

1804–1830 Tasmanian Aboriginal Australians battle British settlers during the Black War.

1976 A law is passed that declares Aboriginal Australians are entitled to their lands.

1850s A gold rush brings many prospectors to Australia. During the rush, many Aboriginal homes and **sacred** sites are destroyed.

1992 Australia's highest court rules that Aboriginal Australians are the original owners of the land.

Social Structures

For most indigenous Australians, religious beliefs are based on a sense of belonging. This comes from the view that all living things are related, which links the idea that every living being was created during the Dreamtime. **Spirituality** is based on being responsible for, and respectful to, the land, the sea, the people, and the Aboriginal culture. For Aboriginal Australians, the land is more than just rocks and grass. It is a whole system that supports life. The land is the center of all spirituality. With spirituality at the center of their social structure, they must respect the land.

Each Aboriginal group tells its own Dreaming stories and is linked to a specific Ancestor Spirit. The paths the spirits traveled during the Dreamtime are of great importance to Aboriginal Australians. These paths marked the territory of a group. Each Aboriginal group has a **totem** figure based on its Ancestor Spirit. A totem can be a plant, animal, or natural object connected to the Dreamtime. For example, people of the kangaroo totem are not allowed to kill or eat kangaroos. They perform special ceremonies in the name of the kangaroo.

Aboriginal Australian children are taught the rules of kinship, which have certain responsibilities. This may include not being allowed to approach some relatives.

On ceremonial occasions, Aboriginal Australians decorate their faces and bodies with paints of different colors. These paints can be made using berries and white clay.

An Aboriginal child is expected to learn these Dreamtime stories and rules at a very early age, so that they can be passed on to future **generations**. Children are taught storytelling techniques and are expected to memorize the stories and songs.

Young Aboriginal Australians learn sacred stories during initiation ceremonies and gatherings. Initiation ceremonies mark the passage of a child into adulthood. For girls, these ceremonies are usually quite simple. For boys, these ceremonies may take several years to complete. They learn the traditions and sacred stories of the group. After a boy completes his final ceremony, he can marry.

While all members of an Aboriginal group are considered equals, the elder members receive the most respect. This is because the elders have the most knowledge to share. Traditional healers often hold a higher status because they are in direct contact with the spirit world. The healer is the link between the Aboriginal world and the spirit world.

THE SEASONS

Aboriginal Australians believe there are as few as two and as many as six seasons, depending on where they live in Australia.

Communication

Identity is very important to an Aboriginal group's survival. Identity comes from the passing of beliefs and traditions from one generation to the next. This is often done through storytelling. Stories are used to educate children about the importance of the land on which they live, how to behave and why, and how to find food and shelter. Starting at a young age, children attend campfire gatherings and take journeys to waterholes, or important landmarks, to listen to stories of their history and culture. When they become adults, it will be their responsibility to pass these stories on to their children. In this way, the identity of a group has been preserved, or kept safe, for thousands of years.

In the past, language was not used to identify different Aboriginal groups. Still, there were differences in the languages they spoke. Most languages spoken by Aboriginal Australians shared basic features. Often, Aboriginal groups that lived close to one another would learn to speak the other group's language. As a result, many Aboriginal Australians were able to speak more than one language.

In some Aboriginal groups, the females pass the traditional stories to the children.

TOAS

Toas were a form of communication, only found in the Lake Eyre region of South Australia. Toas were placed in the ground as signposts to other Aboriginal Australians. When an Aboriginal group moved to another camp, they often left toas behind. These toas would contain directions to the next camp. Toas could also be used to tell stories. Toas were made out of wood and came in many shapes and sizes. Aboriginal Australians used dyes to decorate the toas.

The message stick was an important way for groups that did not speak the same language to communicate. Before entering a new territory, Aboriginal Australians would hold up a message stick carved with their group's totem. These symbols would identify different groups. Using message sticks helped groups communicate and maintain peace. Sign language was necessary for times when it was important to be silent.

For example, it was tradition to be silent during a hunt or during **mourning** and initiation rituals. Instead of speaking, body language and signals were used. Smoke signals were used to communicate over long distances. If two Aboriginal groups were hunting together, one group might send a signal to the other. This signal would represent a message that the groups had agreed on before the hunt.

Aboriginal Australians are well known for their longstanding rock art tradition. The earliest rock engravings date back more than 30,000 years.

Some toas could be shaped like a river, while others might take the form of an animal. Toas shaped like rivers might be used as a map, with a dot marking the spot where an Aboriginal group was camped.

Law and Order

Traditionally, the Aboriginal Australians' relationship with the land governed all actions and behaviors. There were few wars of **conquest**. Each group recognized that different territories were connected to specific Ancestor Spirits. An Aboriginal group would never occupy land that was associated with another group for fear that the spirits would punish them.

Even today, many Aboriginal individuals believe that they must be invited to stay in a particular area. It is believed that if they are not welcome, the spirits will punish them.

In Aboriginal culture, all laws were related to the Dreamtime. For Aboriginal Australians, punishment from spirits was considered far worse than the physical punishment associated with humanmade laws. The Aboriginal culture does not separate the body from the mind and spirit. All are related through creation. As a result, spiritual punishment affected not only the mind and spirit, but also the body. Laws were created by the spirit world and applied by a healer. There were no police forces or governments. To avoid punishment, Aboriginal peoples respected each other and nature.

Aboriginal Australians believe the mind, body, and spirit to be connected. A healer applied their laws. Consequences for breaking them could include the infliction of wounds.

The land is a very important part of Aboriginal spirituality. Aboriginal Australians believe they are connected to the land around them.

Each Aboriginal group lived according to the Dreaming. The laws of the Dreaming explained many things, such as how much food could be eaten, who each group member should marry, and how members should be educated. Special roles were given to each member of the group depending on their age and gender. Traditionally, women gathered food, and men hunted.

All members of a group were considered **kin**. Kinship relations have certain rights and follow specific behaviors. Group members treated each other as though they were family even if they were not actually related through blood or marriage.

Today, Aboriginal Australians' traditional ways of life and law are being combined with newer forms of government and politics. Aboriginal Australians received the right to vote in 1967. This decision gave Aboriginal Australians the ability to represent themselves in political systems. The Office of Aboriginal and Torres Strait Islander Affairs was created to ensure Aboriginal Australians' lands, political, and social needs are being addressed in culturally appropriate ways.

Councils of Aboriginal men often decided matters relating to land and boundaries. They agreed on the locations of common meeting areas where other tribes were allowed.

Celebrating Culture

For thousands of years, Aboriginal Australians have preserved their ancient traditions by living in the same ways as their ancestors. Through sacred ceremonies, Aboriginal Australians celebrate their origins and honor the Dreamtime. They are not allowed to talk or write about many of their ceremonies because they are sacred rituals. However, all ceremonies are related to keeping the stories of the Dreamtime alive. In each community, there are people whose job it is to remember the Dreamtime stories. They must memorize every part of the story and its ceremony to pass on to future generations. During ceremonies, Aboriginal Australians perform the Dreamtime stories. Often, men act as the keeper of a Dreamtime site. Their job is to ensure the area is properly cared for and the Ancestor Spirit is able to continue living at the site. Women act as the keepers of knowledge. They have spiritual and religious power.

Aboriginal Australians hold many different types of ceremonies. Some ceremonies are performed for men only. Others are acted out for women only. Sometimes, Aboriginal Australians hold private ceremonies to which only a few members of a community were invited. Other times, ceremonies are big events involving an entire community.

Music plays an important role in ceremonies. Aboriginal Australians perform sacred songs and dances during ceremonies. They also create sacred symbols such as carvings in wood or clay, **body adornment**, or rock art. Today, bands such Yothu Yindi promote Aboriginal culture by sharing traditional ceremonial music and dances with the world. Yothu Yindi has both Aboriginal and non-Aboriginal members. The musical group combines the sounds of rock and roll music with traditional Aboriginal Australian music that is thousands of years old.

Stories, traditions, and knowledge are passed down from one generation to the next in Aboriginal culture. For example, young boys are taught to hunt at an early age.

The Aboriginal members of the musical group Yothu Yindi come from settlement areas on the northeast coast of Australia's Northern Territory. Yothu Yindi brings Aboriginal Australians' traditions to other cultures by performing songs, dances, and ceremonies.

Art and Culture

Aboriginal Australians use art to express their beliefs and spiritual ideas. Places of worship were chosen because they had a connection to the Dreamtime stories. Places of worship might include an outcropping of rock, a waterhole, or a grove of trees. Much Aboriginal Australian art is inspired by these important places. During traditional **corroborees**, men would paint their bodies with ochers, which are colorful types of earth and mud, and wear emu feathers. Stories were told through song and dance. These were performed to the rhythm of hand clapping and click-sticks. When an important event happened, Aboriginal groups decided how to record the story. Then, it would be memorized and performed.

About 7,000 Aboriginal Australian artists are actively involved in the regular creation of art or crafts.

Aboriginal Australian art is often inspired by nature. This art is made up of painted or engraved images on rock and bark or carved designs into wood. Rock art was the most common art form practiced by Aboriginal Australians. The images of animals, plants, spirits, and totems were painted on caves, cliffs, and rocks. Animals were an important part of Aboriginal culture, and they would often include animal images in their art. The "x-ray" painting technique is an ancient art form depicting the insides of animals and people.

This rock painting, called *Lightning Babies*, is one example of rock art found in caves in the Australian Outback.

Earthworks, wood carvings, and bark paintings told the stories of the spiritual and natural worlds. These drawings included images of animals, landmarks, and people. Aboriginal Australians also used these drawings to record daily events.

The designs of paintings and carvings were filled with wavy lines, circles, curves, and hundreds of small dots. Each pattern told a different story. For example, one pattern that appeared in many drawings was a large circle with smaller circles inside. This pattern was often used to represent a campsite or a house. A squiggly wave pattern was used to represent water or rain. Aboriginal painters used brushes made from the chewed ends of twigs, bundles of grass to splash ochers onto a surface, and finger-painting. These drawings reveal the history, laws, and beliefs of Aboriginal Australian society.

Painting on Rocks

Rock paintings were created using a mixture of pigments. A pigment is any item found in nature that can be crushed and mixed with water to make paint. Black was made from charcoal. White was made using gypsum. Ochers make the most vivid colors, such as red, yellow, and even purple. Pigments were painted on cave walls using feathers and twigs.

Dressing Up

There are many types of ceremonies and rituals in Aboriginal Australian culture. People of all ages take part in them. Aboriginal Australians often paint their faces and bodies for these ceremonies.

Traditionally, Aboriginal Australians were not ashamed of their nakedness. They did not wear clothes during the summer months. Still, some groups wore belts made from animal skin or fur to carry tools. During the winter months, possum and other animal skins were used to make blankets, cloaks, and rugs for warmth. When European settlers arrived, many Aboriginal Australians were forced to cover their bodies and wear old clothing, such as army jackets, dresses, and trousers.

Body adornment has always been an important part of Aboriginal culture. When hunting, men would cover themselves with ashes, branches, and mud to mask their scent. They painted ochers on their bodies to disguise themselves.

There are secret ceremonies for children to which adults are not invited. During these ceremonies, boys decorate their bodies with the symbols of their totem.

The body was also painted for celebrations and initiation rituals. Symbols and designs painted on a body would reveal personal totems and group identity.

During initiation ceremonies, some Aboriginal groups would cut a hole through their noses and wear a bone or a piece of wood through it. Animal bones, fish bones, and feathers were often used to decorate hair. Some Aboriginal groups used scarification to decorate their bodies. Scarification is the practice of creating scars on a person's skin.

Other groups performed scarification during initiation and mourning rituals. Scars were often used as a form of communication. These markings told stories about becoming an adult, losing a loved one, or preparing for marriage. Scars became a part of a person's identity. During rituals and ceremonies, Aboriginal Australians wore headgear. Headgear often had sacred boards and **bullroarers**. One type of headgear was shaped like a cone and topped with feathers. Ritual masks and headgear varied from one group to another. They symbolized the beliefs and traditions of each group.

The designs used by Aboriginal Australians may reflect their social standing and relationship to their family group, particular ancestors, their totem animals, and their land.

BODY TALK

Scarification was a painful ritual that symbolized a rite of passage. Aboriginals began receiving scars at 16 or 17 years of age. Popular places for scars included the back, chest, shoulders, and stomach. Scar patterns were unique to each group and told the story of a person's courage, identity, sorrow, and status. Many Aboriginal groups called people without scars "clean skin" or "unbranded." Aboriginal Australians who did not have scars were not allowed to take part in important rituals. Scarification is no longer practiced in most parts of Australia.

Food and Fun

Traditionally, Aboriginal Australians were hunter-gatherers. They hunted animals and gathered plants for food. Aboriginal Australians had a complete understanding of the foods available in their environment. For example, several Aboriginal groups found a way to eat poisonous plants. They learned how to remove poison from the seeds of **cycad** plants. These seeds were ground into flour to make bread.

Aboriginal Australians from coastal regions ate mainly fish, along with bulrush roots, coconuts, and yams. The inland groups ate a variety of plants and animals. Some common inland foods included kangaroos, ostrich eggs, reptiles, and wallabies. Many Aboriginal groups used fire to clear areas of land. This helped the growth of new grasses and plants. The new growth attracted animals for hunting. At least half of the food eaten by Aboriginal Australians came from plants. In the summer months, they ate many fruits and vegetables.

The Aboriginal Australian Diet

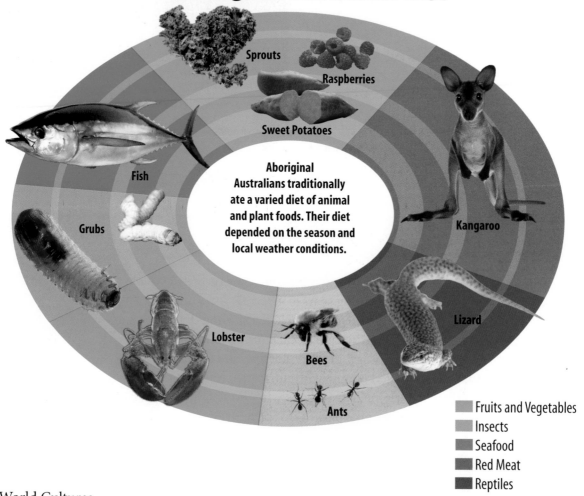

Sprouts

Raspberries

Sweet Potatoes

Fish

Grubs

Aboriginal Australians traditionally ate a varied diet of animal and plant foods. Their diet depended on the season and local weather conditions.

Kangaroo

Lizard

Lobster

Bees

Ants

- Fruits and Vegetables
- Insects
- Seafood
- Red Meat
- Reptiles

In the winter, they ate plant roots. Aboriginal Australians also ate insects, such as ants, bees, grubs, and moths. Insects were used in medicines and foods, too.

For Aboriginal Australians, sports and entertainment were connected to survival and tradition. Children and adults took part in activities such as climbing, jumping, running, and throwing. Games such as skipping and swinging were played for fun. Aboriginal groups competed against one another in contests such as animal tracking, boomerang throwing, swimming, tree climbing, and wrestling. For fun, children often imitated adult activities. Children played with dolls made of twigs and clay. They would pretend to be either the mother or the father. Girls played with smaller versions of their mother's digging sticks. Boys practiced throwing small spears. Aboriginal children often played ball games, climbed trees, and held races. Most activities made use of the natural landscape, such as skipping stones across water surfaces.

Aboriginal Australians made body decorations such as headbands, bracelets, necklaces, and pendants. They also made crafts from animal teeth and bones, feathers, shells, and woven fibers.

Participation in ceremonies and rituals helps young Aboriginal Australians understand their culture's laws and stories.

Grub Recipe

- Dig up the roots of acacia bushes.
- Chop them to get to the witchetty grubs, or larvae.
- Cook the grubs in ashes.

- Grubs add calories, protein, and fat to a meal. Grubs taste similar to almonds.
- Ten large grubs provide enough food for one adult.

Great Ideas

Aboriginal culture is deeply connected to the natural world. Using natural resources, Aboriginal Australians have made many items. These items helped them adapt to their environment. For example, Aboriginal Australians did not live in houses. Instead, during the mosquito season, they built huts of grass and bark. They lit small fires inside the huts to drive the insects away. In windy regions, they built walls of tree and stone, called windbreaks. These windbreaks would shield the village from gusts of wind.

The didgeridoo is a traditional instrument that Aboriginal Australians play during celebrations, corroborees, and rituals. A didgeridoo is a long, cone-shaped, wooden horn. It was made from a branch of a tree that had been hollowed out by termites. The bark was removed from the hollowed branch. Hot coals or a stick were used to clean out the branch. The smaller end of the branch was coated with beeswax to make a mouthpiece. The didgeridoo was painted with the group's designs and totems. A person would blow into the mouthpiece to make a sound.

Didgeridoos are made from trees hollowed out by termites. The harvesting of trees to make this instrument must be carefully timed. This ensures the didgeridoo is the proper thickness.

The sound a didgeridoo made depended on the length and width of the branch. Aboriginal Australians still use the didgeridoo to play songs for different ceremonies. They play Dreaming songs, funeral songs, and hunting songs.

The boomerang is one item that displayed Aboriginal Australians' woodworking skills. The boomerang was a curved, flat, wooden weapon used to hunt and defend. When thrown, the boomerang would soar more than 295 feet (90 meters) in the air. It would then circle around and return to the thrower. This item allowed Aboriginal men to hunt animals from a safe distance. When thrown into a flock of birds, a boomerang looked like a hawk. Often, as the birds tried to escape the hawk, they would fly into the hunter's nets. Aboriginal Australians made many other items from natural resources, such as clubs, digging sticks, shields, spears, and throwing sticks. Many other cultures hunted with non-returning throwing sticks, but the boomerang is unique to Aboriginal Australia.

Aboriginal groups used the boomerang mainly for hunting but also in religious ceremonies. The weapon can easily kill a small animal or knock down a larger one.

The Returning Stick

A boomerang returns to its thrower because of its special design. A boomerang has two wings, which allow it to spin around the center bend. The two wings are designed like the wings of an airplane—the bottoms are flat and the tops are rounded. Air flows differently around the bottom than the top, creating upward lift. When the wings spin, one wing pushes the boomerang forward and one wing pulls it backward. At a certain point, the boomerang stops moving forward and starts moving backward. Not everyone can make a boomerang return. It takes practice to throw it just right.

At Issue

Uluru is the Aboriginal Australian name for the geological sandstone formation also known as Ayers Rock. Uluru is located in Uluru-Kata Tjuta National Park in the Northern Territory. Geologists have estimated the rock to be about 500 million years old.

When European settlers first arrived in Australia, they failed to understand the relationship Aboriginal Australians share with the land. For hundreds of years, this relationship has been misunderstood. This relationship is at the center of all the issues facing Aboriginal Australians today.

When the government forced Aboriginal Australians from their land, their culture and survival were placed in danger. They lost many of the medicines and foods they relied on for survival because they were no longer able to maintain their relationship with the natural world.

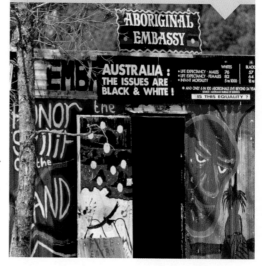

Aboriginal Australian activists often speak out about how government policies affect their people.

In 1938, a group of Aboriginal Australian **activists** gathered to declare a Day of Mourning for the treatment of their people. They wanted to bring attention to the issues affecting them so that all Australian citizens understood their plight. Aboriginal Australians wanted support in seeking the same **civil rights** as the rest of the country's citizens. It took decades to gain some of these rights. In 1962, Aboriginals received the right to vote, and in 1967 they were officially recognized as citizens of Australia. This meant Australia's Commonwealth government would start to take responsibility for Aboriginal Australians.

In 1985, a group of Aboriginal artists created a poster demanding that Ayers Rock and the surrounding area be returned to its original owners, the Aboriginal Australians. Land rights to this tourist attraction were returned, and its name changed to Uluru, the name Aboriginals have used for thousands of years. They believe the rock is the spiritual heart of Australia. In 2004, the Australian government established a National Heritage List that includes protection for other places and items that are sacred to the Aboriginal community.

Today, Aboriginal Australians are asking that their culture and heritage be preserved. They are deeply connected to their whole environment and continue to work to regain land rights, to maintain their traditional beliefs, and ways of life. Laws now exist allowing Aboriginal groups to govern their own territory.

Many organizations have been formed to represent Australia's Aboriginal people. The National Congress of Australia's First Peoples was formed in 2010. It includes a national board of directors led by eight elected men and women, and a six-member ethics council. The group advocates for Aboriginal and Torres Strait Islander people's rights and works to ensure an economic, social, cultural, and environmental future for the people it represents.

The Australian Human Rights Commission works to promote respect and understanding between Aboriginals and other Australian citizens. The commission advocates **social justice** for every Australian.

Australia Day Protest

On January 26, 1988, about 40,000 Aboriginal Australians marched to Sydney Harbour in one of the largest gatherings in the culture's history. It was Australia Day, a day that many Australians mark to celebrate the colonization of Australia by European settlers. It was the 200th anniversary of the settlers' arrival. Aboriginal Australians consider this a day of mourning. They refer to Australia Day as Invasion Day or Survival Day. It is the day when Europeans began taking away their culture, land, and lifestyle. The protest focused worldwide attention on Aboriginal Australian concerns and issues.

Into the Future

Australia's Aboriginals are the country's poorest and most disadvantaged group. Many measures are being taken to improve the situation. In 2011, the Australian Research Council announced funding for 10 Indigenous research teams. Under the Discovery Indigenous program, Aboriginal Australian researchers and research students study issues affecting their community and find solutions to help improve the lives of Aboriginal Australians. One project, for example, focuses on improving mental health, parenting skills, and **resilience** in young Aboriginal parents.

In 2008, the Australian government made a formal apology to Australia's Aborigines for the treatment, pain, and suffering they endured under old laws and policies. By the late 1960s, about 100,000 Aboriginal children had been taken from their parents and **assimilated**. They have come to be known as the "Stolen Generation." It was hoped that the official apology would help heal the relationship between Aboriginal and non-Aboriginal Australians.

Aboriginal Australians have also formed groups to bring attention to issues that affect the community. Some groups cooperate with the government to solve problems or deliver programs that help improve the lives of Aboriginals. The Cathy Freeman Foundation, which oversees educational, sports, activity, and scholarship programs for indigenous children, is one such group. Freeman, a retired Aboriginal track-and-field athlete with many gold medals to her name, formed the foundation in 2007. She wanted to give back to the community that supported her dreams, so that other indigenous children could fulfill their own dreams.

Art also plays an important role as Aboriginal Australians move forward. Traditional art forms are kept alive and modern art forms practiced in the many art centers Aboriginal Australians have built with government support. The Injalak Arts Center in the Northern Territory is one of a number of centers offering supplies and housing to indigenous artists. The art created at these centers is sold to galleries. While artists benefit from sales, the larger community benefits by learning about Aboriginal culture and traditions.

Aboriginal Australians preserve their cultural traditions through art.

Role-play Debate

When people debate a topic, two sides take a different viewpoint about one idea. Each side presents logical arguments to support its views. In a role-play debate, participants act out the roles of the key people or groups involved with the different viewpoints. Role-playing can build communication skills and help people understand how others may think and feel. Usually, each person or team is given a set amount of time to present its case. The participants take turns stating their arguments until the time set aside for the debate is up.

THE ISSUE

The Australian government made a formal apology to Aboriginal Australians for past laws and policies that caused suffering and loss to the Aboriginal people. The Australian government has said that improving life for Aboriginals is one of its top priorities. Many Aboriginals welcomed the apology but argued

that it should have come with an offer of paid compensation to the victims. Only Tasmania, Australia's smallest state, has set up a compensation fund for the Stolen Generations.

THE QUESTION

Should Aboriginal Australians receive paid compensation for the effects that past government decisions have had on their people?

THE SIDES

NO

Government: An apology is enough. We should not have to pay Aboriginal Australians for the decisions, policies, and actions of past governments.

YES

Aboriginal Australians: We, the victims of the Stolen Generation, believe that money will make the apology mean more and will help to improve the lives of those affected by the issue.

Ready, Set, Go

Form two teams to debate the issue, and decide whether your team will play the role of the government or the role of Aboriginal Australians. Each team should take time to use this book and other research to develop solid arguments for its side and to understand how the issue affects each group. At the end of the role-play debate, discuss how you feel after hearing both points of view.

World Cultures Quiz!

1 How long ago did Aboriginal Australians stop being nomadic?

2 According to Aboriginal Australians, when were all things on Earth created?

3 Who claimed the continent of Australia for Great Britain in 1770?

4 What year were Aboriginal Australians allowed to become citizens of Australia?

5 Who are the most respected members of Aboriginal groups?

6 What Aboriginal Olympic athlete now runs a foundation that helps Aboriginal Australian children?

7 What is a didgeridoo?

8 What is the Stolen Generation?

9 Why is Uluru important to Aboriginal Australians?

10 What are the main features of x-ray paintings?

ANSWER KEY

1. 200 years ago **2.** During the Dreamtime **3.** Captain James Cook **4.** 1967 **5.** Elders **6.** Cathy Freeman **7.** A musical instrument made from a tree branch **8.** Aboriginals who were taken from their families as children **9.** They believe it is the spiritual heart of Australia. **10.** Drawing the skeleton and inside of people and animals

Key Words

activists people who believe strongly in political or social change and try to make changes happen

ancestor a person, plant, animal, or object from a past generation

assimilated adopted the customs and views of another culture

banish to force out of a place

billabongs low areas of ground that were once rivers

body adornment decorating the body with colored pigments, scars, or ornaments

bullroarers instruments made from a thin, flat piece of wood attached to a string; makes a howling or roaring sound when it is spun

civil rights the rights given to a person in a society

colony a country or area that is controlled by a more powerful country

conquest to gain control of something

continent one of Earth's seven large areas of land, including Africa, Antarctica, Asia, Australia, Europe, North America, and South America

corroborees celebrations that are usually held at night, at which time Aboriginal Australians tell stories using songs and dances

cycad plants that resemble palms or tree-ferns

earthworks large designs made from raised earth or mud

generations people of the same age living in a society or family

identity the qualities by which a person or group is known

indigenous peoples the first, or original, inhabitants of a particular region or country

initiation ceremonies processes by which someone becomes part of a group

kin family members or relatives

mourning feeling sadness over a person's death

nomadic a tendency to move from place to place

outback the large middle region of Australia that is a dry, semi-desert area

resilience: the ability to adjust or recover from misfortune or change

sacred things that are spiritual, religious, and holy

social justice: equitable distribution of society's benefits and laws

spirituality having deep feelings and beliefs about something that is not part of the physical world

totem an object or being that is the symbol of a group or family; a religious symbol

Index

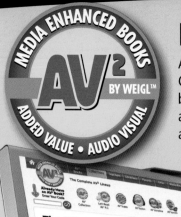

Log on to www.av2books.com

AV² by Weigl brings you media enhanced books that support active learning. Go to www.av2books.com, and enter the special code found on page 2 of this book. You will gain access to enriched and enhanced content that supplements and complements this book. Content includes video, audio, weblinks, quizzes, a slide show, and activities.

Audio
Listen to sections of the book read aloud.

Video
Watch informative video clips.

Embedded Weblinks
Gain additional information for research.

Try This!
Complete activities and hands-on experiments.

WHAT'S ONLINE?

Try This!	Embedded Weblinks	Video	EXTRA FEATURES
Map the area in which Aboriginal Australians live.	Learn more about Aboriginal Australians.	Watch a video about Aboriginal Australian arts and crafts.	**Audio** Listen to sections of the book read aloud.
Write a biography about a well-known Aboriginal Australian person.	Read about the history of Aboriginal Australians.	See how Aboriginal Australians live today.	**Key Words** Study vocabulary, and complete a matching word activity.
Create a timeline showing the history of Aboriginal Australians.	View the arts and crafts of Aboriginal Australians.		**Slide Show** View images and captions, and prepare a presentation
Draw a chart to show the foods Aboriginal Australians eat.			**Quizzes** Test your knowledge.
Test your knowledge of Aboriginal Australians.			

AV² was built to bridge the gap between print and digital. We encourage you to tell us what you like and what you want to see in the future.

Sign up to be an AV² Ambassador at www.av2books.com/ambassador.